PUFFIN BOOKS

Going to the Fair

Charles Causley was born and brought up in Launceston, Cornwall, which is still his home. After six years in the wartime Royal Navy, he became a teacher, before deciding to devote himself to writing full-time. He has published many collections of his own poetry, as well as editing a number of anthologies, and has also written short stories, verse plays and libretti for opera and music-theatre.

He has read his poems in many parts of the world and has acted as Writer-in-Residence at Universities and Arts Centres in Australia and Canada. He is also a frequent broadcaster.

He was awarded the Queen's Gold Medal for Poetry in 1967, is a Fellow of the Royal Society of Literature, and was appointed CBE in 1986. In 1990 he received the Ingersoll/T. S. Eliot Award of America.

Other books by Charles Causley

EARLY IN THE MORNING
FIGGIE HOBBIN
THE PUFFIN BOOK OF MAGIC VERSE (ED.)
THE SUN, DANCING (ED.)
THE TAIL OF THE TRINOSAUR

CHARLES CAUSLEY

Going to the Fair

Selected Poems for Children

Illustrated by Lianne Payne

PUFFIN BOOKS

To
Nell Jacoby

PUFFIN BOOKS

Published by the Penguin Group
Penguin Books Ltd, 27 Wrights Lane, London W8 5TZ, England
Penguin Books USA Inc., 375 Hudson Street, New York, New York 10014, USA
Penguin Books Australia Ltd, Ringwood, Victoria, Australia
Penguin Books Canada Ltd, 10 Alcorn Avenue, Toronto, Ontario, Canada M4V 3B2
Penguin Books (NZ) Ltd, 182–190 Wairau Road, Auckland 10, New Zealand

Penguin Books Ltd, Registered Offices: Harmondsworth, Middlesex, England

First published by Viking1994
Published in Puffin Books 1996
3 5 7 9 10 8 6 4

Text copyright © Charles Causley, 1994
Illustrations copyright © Lianne Payne, 1994
All rights reserved

The moral right of the author has been asserted

Filmset in Palatino

Made and printed in Great Britain by Clays Ltd, St Ives plc

Contents

Out in the Desert

Out in the desert lies the sphinx
It never eats and it never drinx
Its body quite solid without any chinx
And when the sky's all purples and pinx
(As if it was painted with coloured inx)
And the sun it ever so swiftly sinx
Behind the hills in a couple of twinx
You may hear (if you're lucky) a bell that clinx
And also tolls and also tinx
And they say at the very same sound the sphinx
It sometimes smiles and it sometimes winx:

But nobody knows just what it thinx.

The Owl Looked out of the Ivy Bush

The owl looked out of the ivy bush
And he solemnly said, said he,
'If you want to live an owlish life
Be sure you are not like me.

'When the sun goes down and the moon comes
    up
And the sky turns navy blue,
I'm certain to go tu-whoo tu-whit
Instead of tu-whit tu-whoo.

'And even then nine times out of ten
(And it's absolutely true)
I somehow go out of my owlish mind
With a whit-tu whoo-tu too.'

'There's nothing in water,' said the owl,
'In air or on the ground
With a kindly word for the sort of bird
That sings the wrong way round.'

'I might,' wept the owl in the ivy bush,
'Be just as well buried and dead.
You can bet your boots no one gives two hoots!'
'Do I, friend my,' I said.

My Mother Saw a Dancing Bear

My mother saw a dancing bear
By the schoolyard, a day in June.
The keeper stood with chain and bar
And whistle-pipe, and played a tune.

And bruin lifted up its head
And lifted up its dusty feet,
And all the children laughed to see
It caper in the summer heat.

They watched as for the Queen it died.
They watched it march. They watched it halt.
They heard the keeper as he cried,
'Now, roly-poly!' 'Somersault!'

And then, my mother said, there came
The keeper with a begging-cup,
The bear with burning coat of fur,
Shaming the laughter to a stop.

They paid a penny for the dance,
But what they saw was not the show;
Only, in bruin's aching eyes,
Far-distant forests, and the snow.

Tam Snow

(to Kaye Webb)

Who in the bleak wood
Barefoot, ice-fingered,
Runs to and fro?
      Tam Snow.

Who, soft as a ghost,
Falls on our house to strike
Blow after blow?
      Tam Snow.

Who with a touch of the hand
Stills the world's sound
In its flow?
      Tam Snow.

Who holds to our side,
Though as friend or as foe
We never may know?
      Tam Snow.

Who hides in the hedge
After thaw, waits for more
Of his kind to show?
      Tam Snow.

Who is the guest
First we welcome, then
Long to see go?
      Tam Snow.

Maggie Dooley

Old Maggie Dooley
Twice a day
Comes to the Park
To search for the stray,
Milk in a bowl,
Scraps on a tray,
'Breakfast time!' 'Supper time!'
Hear her say.

Alone on a bench
She'll sit and wait
Till out of the bushes
They hesitate:
Tommy No-Tail
And Sammy No-Fur,
Half-Eye Sally
And Emmy No-Purr.

She sits by the children's
Roundabout
And takes a sip
From a bottle of stout.
She smiles a smile
And nods her head
Until her little
Family's fed.

Whatever the weather,
Shine or rain,
She comes at eight
And eight again.
'It's a Saint you are,'
To Maggie I said,
But she smiled a smile
And shook her head.

'Tom and Sammy,
Sally and Em,
They need me
And I need them.
I need them
And they need me.
That's all there is,'
She said, said she.

I Love My Darling Tractor

I love my darling tractor,
I love its merry din,
Its muscles made of iron and steel,
Its red and yellow skin.

I love to watch its wheels go round
However hard the day,
And from its bed inside the shed
It never thinks to stray.

It saves my arm, it saves my leg,
It saves my back from toil,
And it's merry as a skink when I give it a drink
Of water and diesel oil.

I love my darling tractor
As you can clearly see,
And so, the jolly farmer said,
Would you if you were me.

Summer was Always Sun

Summer was always sun,
Winter was made of snow,
Forward the spring, the fall
Was slow.

Down from the moor the stream
Ran swift, ran clear.
The trees were leaved with song
For all to hear.

The seas, the skies were blue.
With stars the beach was sown.
Printing the endless shore,
A child: barefoot, alone.

What is this time, this place?
I hear you say.
When was the wide world so?
Yesterday.

As I Went down Zig Zag

Zig Zag is the name of a steep footpath in Launceston.

As I went down Zig Zag
   The clock striking one,
I saw a man cooking
   An egg in the sun.

        As I went down Zig Zag
           The clock striking two,
        I watched a man walk
           With one boot and one shoe.

As I went down Zig Zag
   The clock striking three,
I heard a man murmuring
   'Buzz!' like a bee.

        As I went down Zig Zag
           The clock striking four,
        I saw a man swim
           In no sea by no shore.

As I went down Zig Zag
   The clock striking five,
I caught a man keeping
   A hog in a hive.

As I went down Zig Zag
The clock striking six,
I met a man making
A blanket of bricks.

As I went down Zig Zag
The clock striking seven,
A man asked me if
I was odd or was even.

As I went down Zig Zag
The clock striking eight,
I saw a man sailing
A seven-barred gate.

As I went down Zig Zag
   The clock striking nine,
I saw a man milking
   Where never were kine.

            As I went down Zig Zag
               The clock striking ten,
            I watched a man waltz
               With a cock and a hen.

As I went down Zig Zag
   The clock striking eleven,
I saw a man baking
   A loaf with no leaven.

            As I went down Zig Zag
               The clock striking twelve,
            For dyes from the rainbow
               I saw a man delve.

So if you'd keep your senses,
   The point of my rhyme
Is don't go down Zig Zag
   When the clocks start to chime.

Simples and Samples

'Simples and samples,' said the White Witch.
'See what I bear in my pack.
Cures for a quinsy and cures for an itch
And one for a crick in the back.

'One for a toothache and one for a rash,
One for a burn or a scald.
One for a colic and one for a gash,
One for a head that is bald.

'One for a pimple and one for a sore,
One for a bruise or a blow.
One for sciatica, one for a snore,
One for a gathering toe.

'One for a nettle sting, one for a bee,
One for the scratch of a briar.
One for a stomach when sailing the sea,
One for St Anthony's fire.'

'White Witch,' I said as she stood in the sun,
'Have you a balm or a brew
For a true loving heart that lately was one
And now is quite broken in two?'

The white old Witch shook me her white old
  head
As down by my side she sat.
'Cures for a thousand, my dear,' she said.
'Never a cure for that.'

A simple is a medicine made from a single herb or plant. St Anthony's fire, also known as 'the rose' or 'the sacred fire', was a name given in earlier times to erysipelas, a fever accompanied by an acute inflammation of the skin. It was a popular belief that cures were possible through the intercession, by prayer, of St Anthony of Padua.

Tommy Hyde

Tommy Hyde, Tommy Hyde,
What are you doing by the salt-sea side?

Picking up pebbles and smoothing sand
And writing a letter on the ocean strand.

Tommy Hyde, Tommy Hyde,
Why do you wait by the turning tide?

I'm watching for the water to rub it off the shore
And take it to my true-love in Baltimore.

Kensey

Here's a card from Tangier, Kensey.
White African air.
Writing on the back says,
'Wish you were here'.

Here's a card from Kashmir, Kensey.
Fretwork mountain, snow.
Writing on the back says,
'Get up and go'.

Here's a card from Eilat, Kensey.
Snorkels, blue glass bay.
Writing on the back says,
'Sun shines all day'.

Here's a card from Rome, Kensey.
The Spanish Steps, flowers.
Writing on the back says,
'Window marked x = ours'.

Tangier, Kashmir, Kensey,
Eilat and Rome.
What say I stir myself?
Stir the fire instead, mister,
Says my old cat Kensey.
Best stay at home.

What Has Happened to Lulu?

What has happened to Lulu, mother?
   What has happened to Lu?
There's nothing in her bed but an old rag-doll
   And by its side a shoe.

Why is her window wide, mother,
   The curtain flapping free,
And only a circle on the dusty shelf
   Where her money-box used to be?

Why do you turn your head, mother,
   And why do the tear-drops fall?
And why do you crumple that note on the fire
   And say it is nothing at all?

I woke to voices late last night,
   I heard an engine roar.
Why do you tell me the things I heard
   Were a dream and nothing more?

I heard somebody cry, mother,
   In anger or in pain,
But now I ask you why, mother,
   You say it was a gust of rain.

Why do you wander about as though
   You don't know what to do?
What has happened to Lulu, mother?
   What has happened to Lu?

How the Sea

'How the sea does shout,'
Says Danny Grout.
'Sounds very vexed.
What does it say?'
Feed me a wreck,
Said Sam-on-the-Shore.

'How the sea cries,'
Says Jimmy Wise.
'Early and late.
What does it say?'
Send me some freight,
Said Sam-on-the-Shore.

'How the sea moans,'
Said Johnnie Stones
Growing pale, then paler.
'What does it say?'
Send me a sailor,
Said Sam-on-the-Shore.

'Shall we sail today?'
Says Dan, says Jim,
Also John.
Don't fancy a cold swim.
Homeward we go, boys.
Put kettle on,
Said Sam-on-the-Shore.

In My Garden

In my garden
Grows a tree
Dances day
And night for me,
Four in a bar
Or sometimes three
To music secret
As can be.

Nightly to
Its hidden tune
I watch it move
Against the moon,
Dancing to
A silent sound,
One foot planted
In the ground.

Dancing tree,
When may I hear
Day or night
Your music clear?
What the note
And what the song
That you sing
The seasons long?

It is written,
Said the tree,
On the pages
Of the sea;
It is there
At every hand
On the pages
Of the land;

Whether waking
Or in dream:
Voice of meadow-grass
And stream,
And out of
The ringing air
Voice of sun
And moon and star.

It is there
For all to know
As tides shall turn
And wildflowers grow;
There for you
And there for me,
Said the glancing
Dancing tree.

Teignmouth

Teignmouth. Ox-red
Sand and scree.
The pier's long finger
Testing the sea.

Salt-damp deck-chairs
Along the Den.
Pierrots singing,
Here we are again!

Sand-artist crimping
The crocodile:
Quartz for a yellow eye,
Shells for a smile.

Punch kills the Baby.
The Mission sings a hymn.
Through the level water
The sailboats swim.

My father, slick
From his boots to his cap,
Driving the Doctor's
Pony and trap.

Here's my mother,
Lives next door,
Strolling with a sun-shade
The long blue shore.

The sun and the day
Burn gold, burn green.
August Bank Holiday,
1914.

In with the evening
The tide runs grey;
Washes a world
Away, away.

Mr Pennycomequick

Mr Hector Pennycomequick
  Stood on the castle keep,
Opened up a carriage-umbrella
  And took a mighty leap.

'Hooray!' cried Mr Pennycomequick
  As he went through the air.
'I've always wanted to go like this
  From here to Newport Square.'

But Mr Hector Pennycomequick
  He never did float nor fly.
He landed in an ivy-bush,
  His legs up in the sky.

Mr Hector Pennycomequick
  They hurried home to bed
With a bump the size of a sea-gull's egg
  On the top of his head.

'So sorry,' said Mr Pennycomequick,
  'For causing all this fuss.
When next I go to Newport Square
  I think I'll take the bus.'

The moral of this little tale
  Is difficult to refute:
A carriage-umbrella's a carriage-umbrella
  And not a parachute.

Mrs Malarkey

Mrs Malarkey
(Miss Rooke, that was)
Climbed to the top of a tree
And while she was there
The birds of the air
Kept her company.

Her friends and her family
Fretted and fumed
And did nothing but scold and sneer
But Mrs Malarkey
She smiled and said,
'I'm perfectly happy up here.

'In this beautiful nest
Of sticks and straw
I'm warmer by far than you,
And there's neither rent
Nor rates to pay
And a quite indescribable view.

'A shield from the snow
And the sun and rain
Are the leaves that grow me round.
I feel safer by far
On this green, green spar
Than ever I did on the ground.'

Mrs Malarkey
She covered herself
With feathers of purple and blue.
She flapped a wing
And began to sing
And she whistled and warbled too.

And the birds of the air
Brought seed and grain
And acorns and berries sweet,
And (I must confirm)
The occasional worm
As an extra special treat.

'Mrs Malarkey!
Come you down!'
The people all cried on the street.
But, *Chirrupy, chirrup*
She softly sang,
And, *Tweet, tweet,*
Tweet, tweet, tweet.
Chirrupy, chirrup
(As smooth as syrup)
And, *Tweet, tweet,*
Tweet, tweet, tweet.

John, John the Baptist

John, John the Baptist
Lived in a desert of stone,
He had no money,
Ate beans and honey,
And he lived quite on his own.

His coat was made of camel,
His belt was made of leather,
And deep in the gleam
Of a twisting stream
He'd stand in every weather.

John, John the Baptist
Worked without any pay,
But he'd hold your hand
And bring you to land
And wash your fears away.

High on the Wall

High on the wall
Where the pennywort grows
Polly Penwarden
Is painting her toes.

One is purple
And two are red
And two are the colour
Of her golden head.

One is blue
And two are green
And the others are the colours
They've always been.

'Quack!' Said the Billy-goat

'Quack!' said the billy-goat.
  'Oink!' said the hen.
'Miaow!' said the little chick
  Running in the pen.

'Hobble-gobble!' said the dog.
  'Cluck!' said the sow.
'Tu-whit tu-whoo!' the donkey said.
  'Baa!' said the cow.

'Hee-haw!' the turkey cried.
  The duck began to moo.
All at once the sheep went,
  'Cock-a-doodle-doo!'

The owl coughed and cleared his throat
  And he began to bleat.
'Bow-wow!' said the cock
  Swimming in the leat.

'Cheep-cheep!' said the cat
  As she began to fly.
'Farmer's been and laid an egg –
  That's the reason why.'

I've Never Seen the Milkman

I've never seen the milkman,
His shiny cap or coat.
I've never seen him driving
His all-electric float.

When he comes by the morning's
As black as printers' ink.
I've never heard his footstep
Nor a single bottle clink.

No matter if it's foggy
Or snow is on the ground,
Or rain or hail or half a gale
He always does his round.

I wonder if he's thin or fat
Or fair or dark or bald,
Or short or tall, and most of all
I wonder what he's called.

He goes to bed so early
That not an owl has stirred,
And rises up again before
The earliest early bird.

God bless the faithful milkman,
My hero – and that's flat!
Or perhaps he's a milklady?
(I never thought of that.)

A Fox Came into My Garden

A fox came into my garden.
'What do you want from me?'
'Heigh-ho, Johnnie-boy,
A chicken for my tea.'

'Oh no, you beggar, and never, you thief,
My chicken you must leave,
That she may run and she may fly
From now to Christmas Eve.'

'What are you eating, Johnnie-boy,
Between two slices of bread?'
'I'm eating a piece of chicken-breast
And it's honey-sweet,' I said.

'Heigh-ho, you diddling man,
I thought that was what I could smell.
What, some for you and none for me?
Give us a piece as well!'

I am the Song

I am the song that sings the bird.
I am the leaf that grows the land.
I am the tide that moves the moon.
I am the stream that halts the sand.
I am the cloud that drives the storm.
I am the earth that lights the sun.
I am the fire that strikes the stone.
I am the clay that shapes the hand.
I am the word that speaks the man.

I Went to Santa Barbara

I went to Santa Barbara,
I saw upon the pier
Four-and-twenty lobster pots
And a barrel of German beer.

The ships in the bay sailed upside-down,
The trees went out with the tide,
The river escaped from the ocean
And over the mountain-side.

High on the hill the Mission
Broke in two in the sun.
The bell fell out of the turning tower
And struck the hour of one.

I heard a hundred fishes fly
Singing across the lake
When I was in Santa Barbara
And the earth began to shake.

My friend Gregor Antonio,
Was with me all that day,
Says it is all inside my head
And there's nothing in what I say.

But I was in Santa Barbara
And in light as bright as snow
I see it as if it were yesterday
Or a hundred years ago.

Why?

Why do you turn your head, Susanna,
And why do you swim your eye?
It's only the children on Bellman Street
Calling, *A penny for the guy!*

Why do you look away, Susanna,
As the children wheel him by?
It's only a dummy in an old top-hat
And a fancy jacket and tie.

Why do you take my hand, Susanna,
As the pointing flames jump high?
It's only a bundle of sacking and straw.
Nobody's going to die.

Why is your cheek so pale, Susanna,
As the whizzbangs flash and fly?
It's nothing but a rummage of paper and rag
Strapped to a stick you spy.

Why do you say you hear, Susanna,
The sound of a last, long sigh?
And why do you say it won't leave your head
No matter how hard you try?

Best let me take you home, Susanna.
Best on your bed to lie.
It's only a dummy in an old top-hat.
Nobody's going to die.

Colonel Fazackerley

Colonel Fazackerley Butterworth-Toast
Bought an old castle complete with a ghost,
But someone or other forgot to declare
To Colonel Fazack that the spectre was there.

On the very first evening, while waiting to dine,
The Colonel was taking a fine sherry wine,
When the ghost, with a furious flash and a flare,
Shot out of the chimney and shivered, 'Beware!'

Colonel Fazackerley put down his glass
And said, 'My dear fellow, that's really first
    class!
I just can't conceive how you do it at all.
I imagine you're going to a Fancy Dress Ball?'

At this, the dread ghost gave a withering cry.
Said the Colonel (his monocle firm in his eye),
'Now just how you do it I wish I could think.
Do sit down and tell me, and please have a
    drink.'

The ghost in his phosphorous cloak gave a roar
And floated about between ceiling and floor.
He walked through a wall and returned through
    a pane
And backed up the chimney and came down
    again.

Said the Colonel, 'With laughter I'm feeling
  quite weak!'
(As trickles of merriment ran down his cheek).
'My house-warming party I hope you won't
  spurn.
You *must* say you'll come and you'll give us a
  turn!'

At this, the poor spectre – quite out of his wits –
Proceeded to shake himself almost to bits.
He rattled his chains and he clattered his bones
And he filled the whole castle with mumbles
  and moans.

But Colonel Fazackerley, just as before,
Was simply delighted and called out, 'Encore!'
At which the ghost vanished, his efforts in vain,
And never was seen at the castle again.

'Oh dear, what a pity!' said Colonel Fazack.
'I don't know his name, so I can't call him back.'
And then with a smile that was hard to define,
Colonel Fazackerley went in to dine.

Python on Piccolo

Python on piccolo,
Dingo on drums,
Gannet on gee-tar*
Sits and strums.

Croc on cornet
Goes to town,
Sloth on sitar
Upside-down.

Toad on tuba
Sweet and strong,
Crane on clarinet,
Goat on gong.
  And the sun jumped up in the morning.

Toucan travelling
On trombone,
Zebra zapping
On xylophone.

Beaver on bugle
Late and soon,
Boa constrictor
On bassoon.

* *guitar*

44

Tiger on trumpet
Blows a storm,
Flying fox
On flügelhorn.
   And the sun jumped up in the morning.

Frog on fiddle,
Hippo on harp,
Owl on oboe
Flat and sharp.

Viper on vibes
Soft and low,
Pelican
On pi-a-no.

Dromedary
On double-bass,
Cheetah on cello
Giving chase.
   And the sun jumped up in the morning.

At Linkinhorne

At Linkinhorne
Where the devil was born
I met old Mollie Magee.
'Come in,' she said
With a wag of her head,
'For a cup of camomile tea.'
And while the water whistled and winked
I gazed about the gloom
At all the treasures Mollie Magee
Had up and down the room.

With a sort of a smile
A crocodile
Swam under an oaken beam,
And from tail to jaw
It was stuffed with straw
And its eye had an emerald gleam.
In the farthest corner a grandfather clock
Gave a watery tick and a tock
As it told the date and season and state
Of the tide at Falmouth Dock.

She'd a fire of peat
That smelled as sweet
As the wind from the moorland high,
And through the smoke
Of the chimney broke
A silver square of sky.
On the mantelshelf a pair of dogs

Gave a china smile and a frown,
And through the bottle-glass pane there stood
The church tower upside-down.

She'd shelves of books,
And hanging on hooks
Were herbals all to hand,
And shells and stones
And animal bones
And bottles of coloured sand.
And sharp I saw the scritch-owl stare
From underneath the thatch
As Matt her cat came through the door
With never a lifted latch.

At Linkinhorne
Where I was born
I met old Mollie Magee.
She told me this,
She told me that
About my family-tree.
And oh she skipped and ah she danced
And laughed and sang did we,
For Mollie Magee's the finest mother
Was ever given to me.

*Linkinhorne is a village in south-east Cornwall, and the first two
lines of the poem are a well-known local saying.*

Jack the Treacle Eater

Here comes Jack the Treacle Eater,
Never swifter, never sweeter,
With a peck of messages,
Some long, some shorter,
From my Lord and Master's quarter
(Built like a minaret)
Somewhere in Somerset.

> *Jack, how do you make such speed*
> *From banks of Tone to banks of Tweed*
> *And all the way back?*
> 'I train on treacle,' says Jack.

Here's one for Sam Snoddy
(Cantankerous old body).
'Will you come for Christmas dinner
With Missus and Squire?'
'Not on your life,' says Sam.
'Rather eat bread and jam
By my own fire.'

> *Jack, how do you trot so spry*
> *The long road to Rye*
> *Bearing that heavy pack?*
> 'I train on treacle,' says Jack.

Here's one for Sally Bent
Lives in a gypsy tent
Down at Land's End.
'Will you sing at my daughter's bridal?'
'No,' says Sally. 'I'm too idle.
Besides, I've not much choice
Since up to Bodmin I lost my voice.'

> *Jack, how do you travel so light*
> *From morning star through half the night*
> *With never a snack?*
> 'I train on treacle,' says Jack.

Here's one for Trooper Slaughter,
Retired, of Petherwin Water.
'Dear Tom, will you come
And we'll talk of our days with the drum,
Bugle, fife and the cannon's thunder.'
'Too late,' says Tom, 'old chum.
I'm already six feet under.'

> *Jack, how do you care for your wife*
> *If you run all the days of your life?*
> *Is it something the rest of us lack?*
> 'I train on treacle,' says Jack.

The original Jack lived in Somerset and was a famous runner who took messages to and from London for the Messiter family of Barwick Park, near Yeovil. He is said to have trained on treacle, and is commemorated there by one of four follies (useless but usually delightful and expensive buildings put up for fun) built by George Messiter in the early nineteenth century. On top of Jack's Folly is a figure of Hermes (representing Jack), the Greek messenger and herald of the gods. At midnight, Jack is said to climb down from his Folly and go to the lake by the great house in order to quench his tremendous thirst, caused by eating so much treacle.

I Saw a Jolly Hunter

I saw a jolly hunter
    With a jolly gun
Walking in the country
    In the jolly sun.

In the jolly meadow
    Sat a jolly hare.
Saw the jolly hunter.
    Took jolly care.

Hunter jolly eager –
    Sight of jolly prey.
Forgot gun pointing
    Wrong jolly way.

Jolly hunter jolly head
    Over heels gone.
Jolly old safety-catch
    Not jolly on.

Bang went the jolly gun.
    Hunter jolly dead.
Jolly hare got clean away.
    Jolly good, I said.

They're Fetching in Ivy and Holly

'They're fetching in ivy and holly
And putting it this way and that.
I simply can't think of the reason,'
Said Si-Si the Siamese cat.

'They're pinning up lanterns and streamers.
There's mistletoe over the door.
They've brought in a tree from the garden.
I do wish I knew what it's for.

'It's covered with little glass candles
That go on and off without stop.
They've put it to stand in a corner
And tied up a fairy on top.

'They're stringing bright cards by the dozen
And letting them hang in a row.
Some people outside in the roadway
Are singing a song in the snow.

'I saw all the children write letters
And – I'm not at all sure this was wise –
They posted each one *up the chimney*.
I couldn't believe my own eyes.

'What on earth, in the middle of winter,
Does the family think it is at?
Won't somebody please come and tell me?'
Said Si-Si the Siamese cat.

How to Protect Baby from a Witch

Bring a bap
Of salted bread
To the pillow
At his head.
Hang a wreath
Of garlic strong
By the cradle
He lies on.
(Twelve flowers
On each stem
For Christ's good men
Of Bethlehem.)
Dress the baby's
Rocking-bed
With the rowan
Green and red.
(Wicked witch
Was never seen
By the rowan's
Red and green.)
Bring the crystal
Water in,
Let the holy
Words begin,
And the priest
Or parson now
Write a cross
Upon his brow.

Mrs McPhee

Mrs McPhee
Who lived in South Zeal
Roasted a duckling
For every meal.

'Duckling for breakfast
And dinner and tea,
And duckling for supper,'
Said Mrs McPhee.

'It's sweeter than sugar,
It's clean as a nut,
I'm sure and I'm certain
It's good for me – BUT

'I don't like these feathers
That grow on my back,
And my silly webbed feet
And my voice that goes quack.'

As easy and soft
As a ship to the sea,
As a duck to the water
Went Mrs McPhee.

'I think I'll go swim
In the river,' said she;
Said Mrs Mac, Mrs Quack,
Mrs McPhee.

At Candlemas

'If candlemas be fine and clear
There'll be two winters in that year';

But all the day the drumming sun
Brazened it out that spring had come,

And the tall elder on the scene
Unfolded the first leaves of green.

But when another morning came
With frost, as Candlemas with flame,

The sky was steel, there was no sun,
The elder leaves were dead and gone.

Out of a cold and crusted eye
The stiff pond stared up at the sky,

And on the scarcely breathing earth
A killing wind fell from the north;

But still within the elder tree
The strong sap rose, though none could see.

Timothy Winters

Timothy Winters comes to school
With eyes as wide as a football pool,
Ears like bombs and teeth like splinters:
A blitz of a boy is Timothy Winters.

His belly is white, his neck is dark,
And his hair is an exclamation mark.
His clothes are enough to scare a crow
And through his britches the blue winds blow.

When teacher talks he won't hear a word
And he shoots down dead the arithmetic-bird,
He licks the patterns off his plate
And he's not even heard of the Welfare State.

Timothy Winters has bloody feet
And he lives in a house on Suez Street,
He sleeps in a sack on the kitchen floor
And they say there aren't boys like him any
    more.

Old Man Winters likes his beer
And his missus ran off with a bombardier,
Grandma sits in the grate with a gin
And Timothy's dosed with an aspirin.

The Welfare Worker lies awake
But the law's as tricky as a ten-foot snake,
So Timothy Winters drinks his cup
And slowly goes on growing up.

At Morning Prayers the Master helves*
For children less fortunate than ourselves,
And the loudest response in the room is when
Timothy Winters roars 'Amen!'

So come one angel, come on ten:
Timothy Winters says 'Amen
Amen amen amen amen.'
Timothy Winters, Lord.
                              Amen.

** a dialect word from north Cornwall used to describe the alarmed
lowing of cattle (as when a cow is separated from her calf); a desperate,
pleading note*

The Young Man of Cury

I am the Young Man of Cury,
I lie on the lip of the sand,
I comb the blown sea with five fingers
To call my true-love to the land.

She gave me a comb made of coral,
She told me to comb the green tide
And she would rise out of the ocean
To lie on the strand by my side.

Her hair flowed about her like water,
Her gaze it was blue, it was bold,
And half of her body was silver
And half of her body was gold.

One day as I lay by the flood-tide
And drew the bright comb to and fro
The sea snatched it out of my fingers
And buried it in the dark flow.

She promised me that she would teach me
All the hours of waking, of sleep,
The mysteries of her salt country,
The runes and the tunes of the deep;

How spells may be broken, how sickness
Be cured with a word I might tell,
The thief be discovered, the future
Be plain as these pebbles, this shell.

My son and his son and his also,
She said, would be heir to such charm
And their lives and their loves hold in safety
For ever from evil and harm.

But never a song does she sing me,
Nor ever a word does she say
Since I carried her safe where the tide-mark
Is scored on the sands of the bay.

I am the Young Man of Cury,
I lie on the lip of the sand,
I comb the blown sea with five fingers
To call my true-love to the land.

Cury is a village near Lizard Point in Cornwall. Cornish legends tell of how a fisherman from Cury rescued a stranded mermaid and returned her to the sea. Robert Hunt has a version called 'The Old Man of Cury' in his Popular Romances of the West of England *(1881), set in Kynance Cove, also in the Lizard peninsula.*

Freddie Phipps

Freddie Phipps
Liked fish and chips.
Jesse Pinch liked crime.

Woodrow Waters
Liked dollars and quarters.
Paul Small liked a dime.

Sammy Fink
Liked a lemon drink.
Jeremy Jones liked lime.

Mortimer Mills
Liked running down hills.
Jack Jay liked to climb.

Hamilton Hope
Liked water and soap.
Georgie Green liked grime;

But Willy Earls
Liked pretty girls
And had a much better time.

Mawgan Porth

Mawgan Porth
The Siamese cat
Lives in an elegant
London flat
Dines on salmon
Sleeps on silk
Drinks Malvern water
Instead of milk
Shops at Harrods
Fortnum & Mason
Has room after room
To run and race in
Wears winter jackets
Of Harris tweed
Strolls in the park
At the end of a lead
But in case you think
As think you might
He's a bit of a drone
Or a parasite
I can tell you quite
Without a qualm
He's a perfectly wonderful
Burglar alarm
For if anyone moves
A bolt or catch
Or touches a single
Security latch
Or worst of all

(I'm certain sure)
Tries to pick the lock
On the big front door
You'll hear him skirl
And you'll hear him squeal
As if his lungs
Were made of steel
You'll hear such a bellow
You'll hear such a blare
As stops the traffic
In Belgrave Square
And for hours and hours
He screeches and squalls
Enough to crack
The dome of St Paul's
Don't you think, I said
To Mawgan Porth
(In his chair that dates
From William IV)
You're a lucky old cat
In this world of strife
To lead such a super-
Superior life?

But nothing he said
As if nothing he knew
Just kept me clearly
Under review
And fixed me firm
With his eyes of blue
His Siamese cat-ical
Aristocratical
Eyes as he gazed me
Through and through.

There was an Old Woman

There was an old woman of Chester-le-Street
Who chased a policeman all over his beat.

She shattered his helmet and tattered his clothes
And knocked his new spectacles clean off his
  nose.

'I'm afraid,' said the Judge, 'I must make it quite
  clear
You can't get away with that sort of thing here.'

'I can and I will,' the old woman she said,
'And I don't give a fig for your water and bread.

'I don't give a hoot for your cold prison cell,
And your bolts and your bars and your
  handcuffs as well.

'I've never been one to do just as I'm bid.
You can put me in jail for year!'
                                   So they did.

Here's the Reverend Rundle

Here's the Reverend Rundle
His gear in a bundle,
He has a dog
He has a sled
And thousands of stories
In his head
And coloured pictures
Of the Holy Scriptures
To show, show
The Indians red
Who had picture and story
And saints in glory
And a heavenly throne
Of their very own
But were so well-bred
That they met him like a brother
And they loved each other
It was said,
The Reverend Rundle
And the Indians red
And through the Rockies
They watched him go
Over the ice
And under the snow –
But this was a very long
Time ago,
A long, long, long, long
Time ago.

They loved him from
His heels to his hat
As he rode on the rough
Or walked on the flat
Whether he stood
Or whether he sat,
The Reverend Rundle
His gear in a bundle
And as well as that
His favourite cat
Warm in a poke
Of his sealskin cloak
For fear some son
Of a hungry gun
Ate her for supper
In Edmonton
And they loved each other
It was said,
The Reverend Rundle
And the Indians red
And through the Rockies
They watched him go
Over the ice
And under the snow –
But this was a very long
Time ago,
A long, long, long, long
Time ago.

When I was a Hundred and Twenty-six

When I was a hundred and twenty-six
And you were a hundred and four
What fun, my dearest dear, we had
At the back of the Co-op store.
It was all such a very long time ago
That it seems just like a dream
In the days when you called me your own Rich
    Tea
And you were my Custard Cream.

Such joys we knew with those dinners *à deux*
At the bottom of the parking lot
On roasted gnu and buffalo stew
And Tandoori chicken in a pot.
Such songs, my love, we used to sing
Till the stars had lost their shine,
And the bells of heaven rang ding, ding, ding
And the neighbours rang 999.

When I was a hundred and twenty-six
And you were a hundred and four
We thought love's cherry would last a very
Long time, and then some more.
But days are fleet when ways are sweet
As the honey in a hive –
And I am a hundred and twenty-seven
And you are a hundred and five.

Who?

Who is that child I see wandering, wandering
Down by the side of the quivering stream?
Why does he seem not to hear, though I call to
him?
Where does he come from, and what is his
name?

Why do I see him at sunrise and sunset
Taking, in old-fashioned clothes, the same
track?
Why, when he walks, does he cast not a shadow
Though the sun rises and falls at his back?

Why does the dust lie so thick on the hedgerow
By the great field where a horse pulls the
plough?
Why do I see only meadows, where houses
Stand in a line by the riverside now?

Why does he move like a wraith by the water,
Soft as the thistledown on the breeze blown?
When I draw near him so that I may hear him,
Why does he say that his name is my own?

Old Billy Ricky

Old Billy Ricky
Lives down a well
Snug as a silver
Snail in a shell,
Sits all day
On a mossy shelf
Keeping himself
(He says) to himself,
Whistles and watches
The circle of sky
As weathers and seasons
Pass him by.

Nothing to eat
But plenty to drink,
How can he ever
Sleep a wink,
Back pressed tight
To a ferny wall
Nothing to catch him
If he should fall,
And what for mercy's
Sake can he see
In a newt and a frog
For company?

But there he sits
In his round stone room
The green moss glimmering
In the gloom,

And if you should ask
On the village square
How long Billy's
Been down there
There's nobody knows
Wherefore or why
And if you ask *him*
You won't get a reply:
He simply won't answer,
He never will tell
Won't old Billy Ricky.

Well! Well! Well!

Good Morning,
Mr Croco-doco-dile

Good morning, Mr Croco-doco-dile,
And how are you today?
I like to see you croco-smoco-smile
In your croco-woco-way.

From the tip of your beautiful croco-toco-tail
To your croco-hoco-head
You seem to me so croco-stoco-still
As if you're croco-doco-dead.

Perhaps if I touch your croco-cloco-claw
Or your croco-snoco-snout,
Or get up close to your croco-joco-jaw
I shall very soon find out.

But suddenly I croco-soco-see
In your croco-oco-eye
A curious kind of croco-gloco-gleam,
So I just don't think I'll try.

Forgive me, Mr Croco-doco-dile
But it's time I was away.
Let's talk a little croco-woco-while
Another croco-doco-day.

On the Eve of St Thomas

On the Eve of St Thomas
I walked the grey wood
Though mammy she told me
That I never should,

And there did I meet
(Though never one spoke)
Kit-with-the-Canstick,*
The Man in the Oak,

Tom Tumbler and Boneless
And Whistle-the-Fife,
Derrick and Puddlefoot,
Gooseberry Wife,

Changeling, Hob Goblin,
Bull-Beggar and Hag,
Tom Thumb and Puckle,
Long-Jack-with-the-Bag.

They nidded and nodded
And winked me an eye,
They bent and they bowed to me
As I passed by.

* *candlestick*

Was never a shudder
Nor ever a scream,
The wood was as silent
As it were a dream.

Though still were their voices
Their lips told me clear
They wished me Good Christmas
And many a year.

They never did blatter
Nor shiver nor shriek,
Nor clamour nor yammer
Nor rustle nor screak

As they pointed my path
By bramble and brake,
Waved each a pale hand
As my leave I did take.

And I thought I could tell
As I said them goodbye
Though their lips they did smile
That sad was each eye

As out the grey wood
I went on my way
To hearth and to home
And St Thomas's Day.

In ancient times it was believed that goblins and ghosts of all kinds were
likely to be seen particularly between St Thomas's Eve (20 December) and
Christmas Eve.

For a Moment Rare

For a moment rare
They looked at it there
With its antique glance
And its three-pronged stance,
And from hill to hill
All the folk stood still
As the trino vast
From the living past
Seemed to stare
  And glare
    And leer
      And peer
        And glint
          And squint
  Both here and there
From its crystal lair.

Though its head not a mite
Moved to left nor right,

Its eye seemed to follow you
Everywhere
With expression strange
That seemed to change
With the shifting
Drifting
Light of day.

And it looked at them all
As if to say,
'Good afternoon –
I'm yesterday.'

from *The Tail of the Trinosaur*

Mary, Mary Magdalene

On the south wall of the church of St Mary Magdalene at Launceston in Cornwall is a granite figure of the saint. The children of the town say that a stone lodged on her back will bring good luck.

Mary, Mary Magdalene
Lying on the wall,
I throw a pebble on your back.
Will it lie or fall?

Send me down for Christmas
Some stockings and some hose,
And send before the winter's end
A brand-new suit of clothes.

Mary, Mary Magdalene
Under a stony tree,
I throw a pebble on your back.
What will you send me?

I'll send you for your Christening
A woollen robe to wear,
A shiny cup from which to sup,
And a name to bear.

Mary, Mary Magdalene
Lying cool as snow,
What will you be sending me
When to school I go?

I'll send a pencil and a pen
That write both clean and neat.
And I'll send to the schoolmaster
A tongue that's kind and sweet.

Mary, Mary Magdalene
Lying in the sun,
What will you be sending me
Now I'm twenty-one?

I'll send you down a locket
As silver as your skin,
And I'll send you a lover
To fit a gold key in.

Mary, Mary Magdalene
Underneath the spray,
What will you be sending me
On my wedding-day?

I'll send you down some blossom,
Some ribbons and some lace,
And for the bride a veil to hide
The blushes on her face.

Mary, Mary Magdalene
Whiter than the swan,
Tell me what you'll send me,
Now my good man's dead and gone.

I'll send to you a single bed
On which you must lie,
And pillows bright where tears may light
That fall from your eye.

Mary, Mary Magdalene
Now nine months are done,
What will you be sending me
For my little son?

I'll send you for your baby
A lucky stone, and small,
To throw to Mary Magdalene
Lying on the wall.

What Happened

What happened to Jonathan Still,
Cider-sour, all smothered in flour,
Used to work Ridgegrove Mill?
> *Off on a long stay*
> *With gran and grand, they say,*
> *Under the hill.*

Never seem to see Tom Black –
Marched with the men, nineteen-I-don't-know-
  when –
With rifle and pack.
> *Showed his soldier face*
> *In some foreign space.*
> *Never came back.*

Where's Silly Dick Sloppy, so small, so slim,
Used to mooch by with rod, basket and fly
To doze on the river brim?
> *Trying the water*
> *This year and a quarter,*
> *Taking a deep swim.*

Do you know where is Tamasine Long,
Her with the green stare, the guinea-gold hair?
Went wandering with Singing Ben Strong?
>   *Never returned –*
>   *Maybe she learned*
>   *A different song.*

What happened to Fidgety Goodge, Tinker
  John,
Little Tim Spy, him with the bad eye,
Beulah and Billy Fireworks, kept The Swan?
>   *Couldn't keep track of 'em,*
>   *Never one of the pack of 'em.*
>   *All gone, gone.*

Pepper and Salt

Pepper and salt his whiskers,
Pepper and salt his hair,
Pepper and salt the three-piece suit
He always likes to wear.

Pepper and salt his muffler,
His hat, and furthermore
Pepper and salt his overcoat
That hangs behind the door.

Pepper and salt his voice is,
Pepper and salt his eye
As he reads out the register
And we pepper and salt reply.

Pepper and salt his singing
When he rises from his chair
And sets to work with a tuning-fork
And a pepper and salty prayer.

He peppers and salts the blackboard
With every kind of sum,
The names of the British Kings and Queens
And the order in which they come.

With a pepper and salty finger
He stabs the maps and charts
And shows us capes and rivers and straits
In home and foreign parts.

Pepper and salt his spectacles,
And it's peppery salty plain
That pepper and salt is his hand of chalk
And pepper and salt his cane.

But silent now the school bell
That Pepper and Salt would sound,
And vanished is the school to which
We came from miles around.

And we who were village children,
Now white of head or hair,
Can never go down the Old School
    Lane
But Pepper and Salt is there –

Standing in the school-yard
Where weeds and grasses win:
Every day, old Pepper and Salt
Seeing the children in.

The Song of Kruger the Cat

I really hate the coalman.
I hate his hood and sack.
I'm sure one day he'll carry me off
In a bundle on his back.

When he crunches up to the bunker
And I hear the coal go *crump*
My legs turn into custard
And my heart begins to bump.

I'm not afraid of a bulldog,
A gull or a giant rat,
The milkman or the postman,
Or the plumber, come to that.

But when I hear the coalman
I shake and quake with fright,
And I'm up and away for the rest of the day
And sometimes half the night.

I'm certain that to his family
He's loving and good and kind,
But when I hear his hobnailed boots
I go right out of my mind.

'Now Kruger, dear,' they say, 'look here:
Isn't it rather droll?
You love to sleep and snore before
A *fire* that's made of coal.'

But I can't help my feelings
However hard I try.
I really hate the coalman.
Who's that? Good grief! Good-bye!

Riverside

When you were born at Riverside,
My mother said to me,
It rained for nights, it rained for days
And then some more, said she.

And all at once came riding
The water with a roar
Along the river valley
Down from Bodmin Moor.

The water came in at the window,
It came in at the door,
It swallowed up the cellar,
It came up through the floor.

It filled up every kettle,
It filled up every crock,
It swam around the fireplace,
It filled the long-case clock.

It climbed the kitchen dresser,
It climbed the kitchen chairs,
It climbed up on the table,
It climbed the kitchen stairs.

And as we wailed and wondered
If we should sink or float,
My father came to Riverside
In a sailing-boat.

He took me and my mother
To move upon the swell,
My brother Shem, my brother Ham,
Their families as well.

He took him food and fodder
To sail upon the blue,
He took aboard all creatures
By two and two and two.

And after days and after nights
Watching the waters pour,
We landed on a mountain-top
Somewhere by Wise Man's Tor.

All this, my mother told me,
Was when I was in my pram,
And next door lived my brother Shem,
And next to him lived Ham.

This tale my mother told me
The truth that I might say
Of when I lived at Riverside
Yesterday.

I Saw Charlie Chaplin

I saw Charlie Chaplin
In 1924
Playing golf with a walking-cane
Outside our front door.

His bowler was a size too early,
His trousers were a size too late,
His little moustache said one o'clock,
His boots said twenty-past eight.

He whacked at a potato.
It broke in the bouncing air.
'Never mind, Charlie,' I said to him.
'We've got some to spare.'

I fetched him out a potato.
He leaned on his S-shaped cane.
'Thanks, kid.' He bowed. He shrugged.
I never saw him again.

My father said Charlie Chaplin
Wasn't Charlie at all.
He said it was someone in our town
Going to a Fancy Ball.

He said it couldn't be Charlie.
That it was Carnival Day.
That Charlie never came to our town,
And he lived in the USA.

Not Charlie Chaplin?
You can tell that tale to the cat.
I don't care what my father said.
I know better than that:

For I saw Charlie Chaplin
Outside our front door
Playing golf with a walking-cane.
It was 1924.

Tavistock Goose Fair

The day my father took me to the Fair
Was just before he died of the First War.
We walked the damp, dry-leaved October air.
My father was twenty-seven and I was four.

The train was whistles and smoke and dirty
   steam.
I won myself a smudge of soot in the eye.
He tricked it out as we sat by a windy stream.
Farmers and gypsies were drunken-dancing by.

My dad wore his Irish cap, his riding-coat.
His boots and leggings shone as bright as a star.
He carried an ashling stick, stood soldier-
   straight.
The touch of his hand was strong as an iron bar.

The roundabout played 'Valencia' on the
    Square.
I heard the frightened geese in a wicker pen.
Out of his mouth an Indian man blew fire.
There was a smell of beer; cold taste of rain.

The cheapjacks bawled best crockery made of
    bone,
Solid silver spoons and cures for a cold.
My father bought a guinea for half-a-crown.
The guinea was a farthing painted gold.

Everyone else was tall. The sky went black.
My father stood me high on a drinking-trough.
I saw a man in chains escape from a sack.
I bothered in case a gypsy carried me off.

Today, I hardly remember my father's face;
Only the shine of his boot-and-legging leather
The day we walked the yellow October weather;
Only the way he strode at a soldier's pace,
The way he stood like a soldier of the line;
Only the feel of his iron hand on mine.

*The Fair is still held every year at this Devonshire town on the second
Wednesday in October.*

Morwenstow

Where do you come from, sea,
To the sharp Cornish shore,
Leaping up to the raven's crag?
    From Labrador.

Do you grow tired, sea?
Are you weary ever
When the storms burst over your head?
    Never.

Are you hard as a diamond, sea,
As iron, as oak?
Are you stronger than flint or steel?
    And the lightning stroke.

Ten thousand years and more, sea,
You have gobbled your fill,
Swallowing stone and slate!
    I am hungry still.

When will you rest, sea?
    When moon and sun
    Ride only fields of salt water
    And the land is gone.

Francesco de la Vega

Francesco de la Vega
From the hours of childhood
Passed his days
In the salt of the ocean.

Only one word he spoke.
Lierjanes! – the name
Of the sea-village of his birth
In the Year of God 1657.

While other children
Helped in field or kitchen,
Wandered the mountain-slope,
He swam the wild bay.

While others were at church
He dived to where lobster and squid
Lodged in the sea's dark cellar.
He must suffer a salt death, said Father Ramiro.

His mother and father entreated him
To come to his own bed.
His brothers and sisters called him
Home from the yellow sand-bar.

Amazed, they watched him
Arrow the waves like a young dolphin.
Until they tired of waiting, he hid
Under the mountain of black water.

On a night mad with storm
The waves rose high as the church-tower
And beat the shore like a drum.
He did not return with the morning.

Foolish boy, now he is drowned, they said.
His family added their salt tears to the ocean
As they cast on flowers and prayers.
In my opinion, he asked for it, said Father Ramiro.

Years flowed by: ten, twenty.
The village of Lierjanes forgot him.
Then, miles off Cadiz, herring fishermen
Sighted, at dawning, a sea-creature.

Three days they pursued him
Through the autumn waters;
Trapped him at last in strong nets
And brought him to land.

They gazed at his silver body in wonder;
At his pale eyes, staring always ahead;
At his hair, tight, and as a red moss.
What seemed like bright scales adorned his
    spine.

Most marvellous of all, instead
Of nails upon his feet and hands
There grew strange shells
That glowed gently like jewels of the sea.

When they questioned him
All he would reply was, *Lierjanes!*
Wrapping him in a soft white sailcloth
They laid him on a bed of linen.

A monk of Cadiz heard their story.
It is Francesco de la Vega,
The fish-boy of Lierjanes, he declared.
I shall bring him to his home and family.

Ah, but how his parents, brothers, sisters
Wept with happiness and welcomed him
With loving kisses and embraces, as though
Like Lazarus he had risen, and from a sea-grave!

But the young man returned no sign
Of love or recognition.
He gazed at them as though sightless;
Was indifferent to their sighs, their fondlings.

Long years he dwelt among them,
Never speaking, eating little,
Shifting unhappily in the decent clothes
With which they arrayed him.

One morning, nine years on,
He vanished from the house and hearth-side;
Was seen no more in the village of Lierjanes.
Great was the sadness of those who loved him!

Months, years ahead, two fishermen
Hauling across the stubborn waters
Of the Bay of Asturias
Sighted a sudden sea-creature at play.

Swiftly, and with spear and net,
They followed, but he escaped them.
As he rushed through the waves they heard a
    cry.
Lierjanes! Lierjanes!

Driving Home

Driving home, in wrong weather,
Half-melted stars adrift
In a warmth of sky, the tin voice
Of the car radio sprinkling
Music for Spanish guitar,
I had forgotten, for some reason,
Time, place and season.

Then, suddenly, the church:
Lit granite lantern.
Coloured glass saints pointing
Stiff arms to pray or praise.
Over its ragged screen
Of elm, yew, oak,
The tower spoke.

As if at the push of dark
The door unclosed.
Men, women, children
In smiling light
Streamed a thin path between
Tomb and long-planted stone.
Headed for home.

Above, six bells (one cracked)
Thumped down the scale.
'Merry Christmas!' Tom, Jack
And Maisie called.
'Don't seem like Christmas.
More like Midsummer,'
They grinned one to another.

'Every day Christmas Day!'
They smelt of whisky and tobacco.
Climbed into the bent, half-spent van,
Making for Moor Farm
As I wondered what,
In all that Mediterranean air,
They should discover there.

By St Thomas Water

By St Thomas Water
Where the river is thin
We looked for a jam-jar
To catch the quick fish in.
Through St Thomas Churchyard
Jessie and I ran
The day we took the jam-pot
Off the dead man.

On the scuffed tombstone
The grey flowers fell,
Cracked was the water,
Silent the shell.
The snake for an emblem
Swirled on the slab,
Across the beach of sky the sun
Crawled like a crab.

'If we walk,' said Jessie,
'Seven times round,
We shall hear a dead man
Speaking underground.'
Round the stone we danced, we sang,
Watched the sun drop,
Laid our heads and listened
At the tomb-top.

Soft as the thunder
At the storm's start
I heard a voice as clear as blood,
Strong as the heart.
But what words were spoken
I can never say,
I shut my fingers round my head,
Drove them away.

'What are those letters, Jessie,
Cut so sharp and trim
All round this holy stone
With earth up to the brim?'
Jessie traced the letters
Black as coffin-lead.
'He is not dead but sleeping,'
Slowly she said.

I looked at Jessie,
Jessie looked at me,
And our eyes in wonder
Grew wide as the sea.
Past the green and bending stones
We fled hand in hand,
Silent through the tongues of grass
To the river strand.

By the creaking cypress
We moved as soft as smoke
For fear all the people
Underneath awoke.
Over all the sleepers
We darted light as snow
In case they opened up their eyes,
Called us from below.

Many a day has faltered
Into many a year
Since the dead awoke and spoke
And we would not hear.
Waiting in the cold grass
Under a crinkled bough,
Quiet stone, cautious stone,
What do you tell me now?

Give Me a House

Give me a house, said Polly.
Give me land, said Hugh.
Give me the moon, said Sadie.
Give me the sun, said Sue.

Give me a horse, said Rollo.
Give me a hound, said Joe.
Give me fine linen, said Sarah.
Give me silk, said Flo.

Give me a mountain, said Kirsty.
Give me a valley, said Jim.
Give me a river, said Dodo.
Give me the sky, said Tim.

Give me the ocean, said Adam.
Give me a ship, said Hal.
Give me a kingdom, said Rory.
Give me a crown, said Sal.

Give me gold, said Peter.
Give me silver, said Paul.
Give me love, said Jenny,
Or nothing at all.

Nursery Rhyme of Innocence and Experience

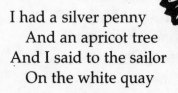

I had a silver penny
    And an apricot tree
And I said to the sailor
    On the white quay

'Sailor O sailor
    Will you bring me
If I give you my penny
    And my apricot tree

'A fez from Algeria
    An Arab drum to beat
A little gilt sword
    And a parakeet?'

And he smiled and he kissed me
    As strong as death
And I saw his red tongue
    And I felt his sweet breath

'You may keep your penny
    And your apricot tree
And I'll bring your presents
    Back from sea.'

O the ship dipped down
  On the rim of the sky
And I waited while three
  Long summers went by

Then one steel morning
  On the white quay
I saw a grey ship
  Come in from sea

Slowly she came
  Across the bay
For her flashing rigging
  Was shot away

All round her wake
  The seabirds cried
And flew in and out
  Of the hole in her side

Slowly she came
  In the path of the sun
And I heard the sound
  Cf a distant gun

And a stranger came running
   Up to me
From the deck of the ship
   And he said, said he

'O are you the boy
   Who would wait on the quay
With the silver penny
   And the apricot tree?

'I've a plum-coloured fez
   And a drum for thee
And a sword and a parakeet
   From over the sea.'

'O where is the sailor
   With bold red hair?
And what is that volley
   On the bright air?

'O where are the other
   Girls and boys?
And why have you brought me
   Children's toys?'

Moor-hens

Living by Bate's Pond, they
(Each spring and summer day)
Watched among reed and frond
The moor-hens prank and play.

Watched them dip and dive,
Watched them pass, re-pass,
Sputtering over the water
As if it were made of glass.

Watched them gallop the mud
Bobbing a tail, a head;
Under an April stream
Swimming with tails outspread.

Listened at night for a cry
Striking the sky like a stone;
The *kik! kik! kik!* of farewell
As they drifted south for the sun.

Whose are the children, and who
Are the children who lived by the pond,
Summer and spring year-long
When the wild sun shone?
Thirsty the stream, and dry;
Ah, and the house is gone.

Index of First Lines